First published by Parragon in 2012

Parragon
Queen Street House
4 Queen Street
Bath BA1 1HE, UK
www.parragon.com

Copyright © Parragon Books Ltd 2012
Text © Hollins University

ISBN 978-1-4454-9327-5

Printed in China

Around the World We Go!

Bath · New York · Singapore · Hong Kong · Cologne · Delhi
Melbourne · Amsterdam · Johannesburg · Shenzhen

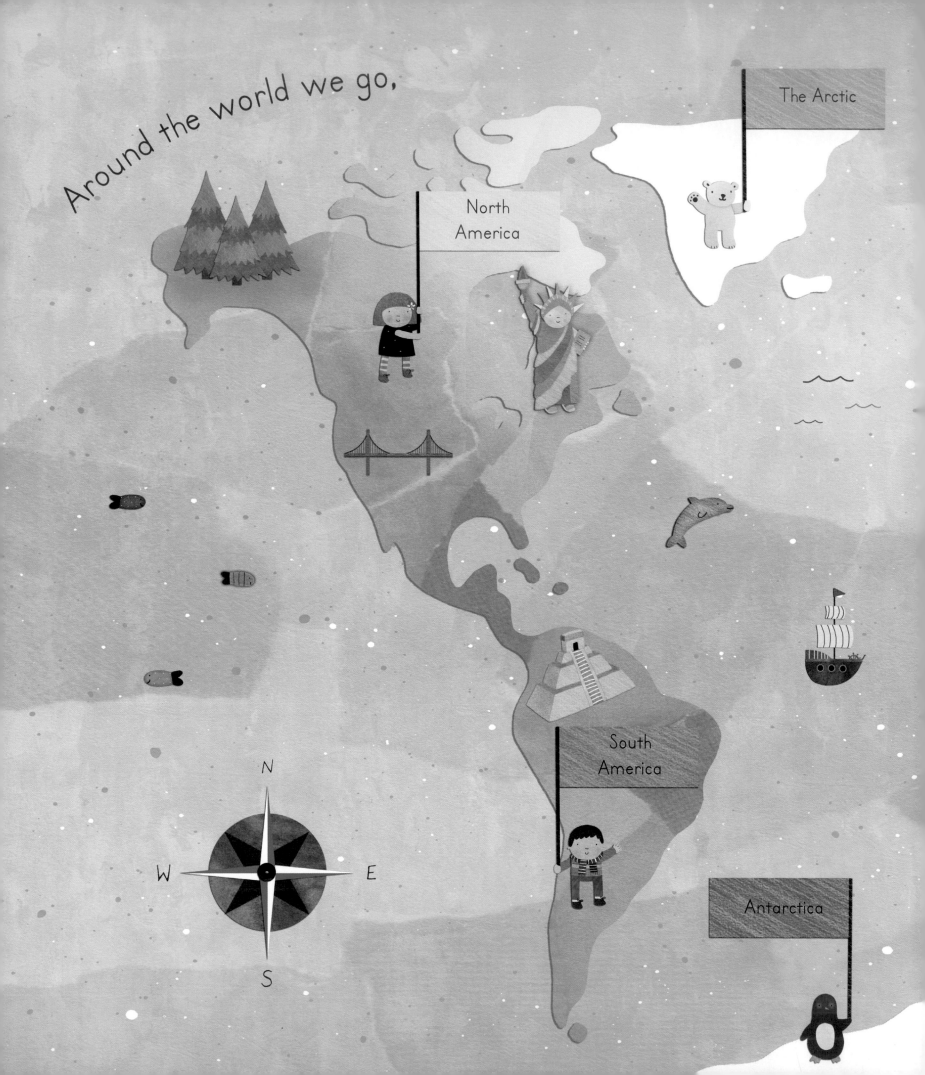

Around the world we go,

The Arctic

North America

South America

Antarctica

N
W E
S

Europe

Asia

Africa

Australia

To learn what we don't know.

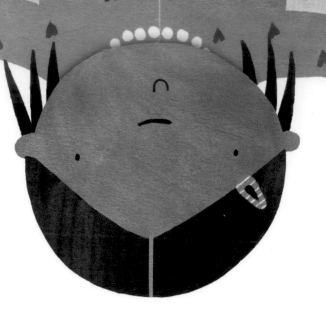

In foreign lands,

We'll all

shake
hands,

As around the world we go!

Around the
world we go,

To learn what we don't know.

We'll make our eyes
A great big size

To see
what we
don't know.

Around the world we go,

Each language we don't know.

But we'll talk too,

Comment ça va?

¿Cómo estás?

How are you?

Around the world we go,

In singing we can show

A way to play

In a friendly way,

As around the world we go.

Around the world we go,

The world is rather slow,

Because we run

ahead of the world,

As around

we

the world
go!